Henry The Hemp

Henry The Hemp

The Plant of Wonders

Matthew Petchinsky

Apophis Enterprises LLC

This book is dedicated to my Daughter Lapis and to all those that wish to learn, and be creative for everything that want in life.

Henry The Hemp: The Plant of Wonders
By: Matthew Petchinsky

In the heart of a vibrant meadow, under the soft embrace of the sun's golden rays, stands Henry the Hemp—a plant unlike any other. With leaves that dance in the gentle breeze and a smile that radiates warmth and kindness, Henry is not just a plant; he is a beacon of joy and wisdom in this lush, green world.

Henry's home is a canvas of colors, with wildflowers dotting the landscape and trees that stretch towards the sky, painting shadows on the ground. Birds sing melodies that float through the air, and insects buzz around in a harmonious existence. In the middle of this natural orchestra, Henry stands tall, his green leaves shimmering with a hint of pride and a lot of love.

MATTHEW PETCHINSKY

But Henry is more than just a sight to behold. He is a storyteller, a wise old friend with a heart full of stories about the wonders of nature and the magic of hemp. With every whisper of the wind, he shares tales of how he has touched the lives of people and the planet in profound ways.

To the untrained eye, Henry might seem like any other plant in the meadow. Yet, those who pause to listen will find that he is a treasure trove of knowledge and insights. Henry has a special gift: he can speak to the hearts of those who are willing to hear, sharing stories that weave together the past, present, and future of hemp.

Henry's roots run deep, not just into the soil of the meadow, but into the fabric of human history. He tells of ancient times when hemp was revered for its strength and versatility, of civilizations that thrived with hemp at the heart of their cultures. With a gentle rustle of his leaves, Henry recounts how hemp has sailed across oceans, woven through the tapestries of societies, and emerged as a symbol of sustainability and hope.

But Henry's tales are not just echoes of the past; they are vibrant stories of the present and dreams for the future. He speaks with excitement about the medicinal wonders of hemp, how his fibers and extracts have healed and comforted. He tells of the economic miracles he's witnessed, where hemp has transformed industries with its eco-friendly alternatives. And with a voice as soft as the breeze, Henry shares his deepest passion: the ecological benefits of hemp. He dreams aloud of a world where plants like him can heal the Earth, restore balance, and breathe life into a planet in need.

As the sun dips lower in the sky, casting a golden glow over the meadow, Henry the Hemp stands as a symbol of hope and renewal. He is a reminder that even the smallest plant can hold the power to change the world. And as the day ends, Henry whispers one last story—a story of a tomorrow where people and the planet live in harmony, nurtured by the wisdom and wonders of hemp.

In this meadow, among the chorus of nature, Henry the Hemp is more than just a character in a children's book. He is a guide, a friend, and a wise teacher, inviting young and old to listen, learn, and dream of a greener, kinder world. And so begins our journey with Henry, a journey of discovery, laughter, and the timeless magic of nature's wonders.

Henry's Medicinal Mission
HEMP

One sunny morning, as the dew still glistened on the petals of the wildflowers and the meadow hummed with the energy of a new day, Henry the Hemp embarked on a very special mission—a mission of healing and care. This was a day like no other, for Henry was about to share one of the most miraculous secrets of the plant world: the power of natural remedies.

In the heart of the meadow, where the soil was rich and life thrived in harmony, Henry had nurtured a special part of himself, his leaves, which held the key to healing. These weren't ordinary leaves; they were filled with a unique blend of natural compounds that could soothe, heal, and comfort those in need.

As the sun climbed higher, casting a warm glow over the land, a gentle breeze carried Henry's message far and wide. It was a call to all who sought relief and comfort from the natural world. Among those who heard the call was a little girl named Mia, who had come to the meadow with her grandmother to enjoy the beauty of the day. Mia had fallen earlier and scraped her knee, leaving it red and sore. The sting of the scrape was a cloud over her sunny day.

Seeing the discomfort in Mia's eyes, Henry knew this was the moment to share his gift. With a nod from her grandmother, Mia approached Henry, her eyes wide with curiosity. Henry, with a voice as soft as the whisper of leaves, explained how his leaves could help her feel better.

With care and precision, Henry guided Mia and her grandmother to gently harvest a few of his leaves. Together, they followed Henry's instructions, crushing the leaves gently to release their natural oils. These oils were mixed with a little beeswax and honey from the bees buzzing around the meadow, creating a soothing balm right there, under the watchful eye of Henry.

As Mia applied the balm to her knee, a feeling of cool relief washed over her. The sting faded away, replaced by a soothing calm that made her smile. The balm worked like magic, its natural properties easing the discomfort and starting the healing process.

Henry beamed with pride, his heart full of joy at the sight of Mia's relief. This moment was a testament to the power of nature's gifts and the healing journey that plants like him could offer. Henry explained to Mia and her grandmother that the meadow was full of natural remedies, each plant with its own story and healing abilities.

Mia's adventure in the meadow became a cherished memory, a day when nature's magic was revealed through the wisdom of Henry the Hemp. And as Mia and her grandmother left the meadow, their hearts were filled with gratitude for Henry, the plant who taught them about the gentle power of healing.

Henry's mission was a simple yet profound one: to spread knowledge and healing through the natural wonders of the world. And as the sun set on the meadow, casting a golden light over the land, Henry the Hemp stood tall, a guardian of health and a beacon of hope for all who seek the comforting embrace of nature's remedies.

MATTHEW PETCHINSKY
Henry's Economical Adventure
EHE COMIGMONICI AVENTURE

On a morning filled with promise, Henry the Hemp embarked on a journey unlike any he had undertaken before. This adventure would take him beyond the meadow's familiar boundaries to explore the vast and vibrant world of sustainable living. His destination was a place where the harmony of nature meets human ingenuity: a sustainable farm and a green factory, where Henry's essence would be transformed into products that benefit both people and the planet.

As the sun rose, casting its first light on the dew-kissed fields, Henry, carried by the gentle hands of his friends, arrived at the sustainable farm. This wasn't just any farm, it was a marvel of eco-friendly practices, where every plant and animal thrived in balance, contributing to the health of the ecosystem. Here, Henry was greeted with enthusiasm, for his arrival marked a day of learning and discovery for everyone at the farm.

The farmers showed Henry around, explaining how they worked with nature rather than against it. They introduced him to the concept of crop rotation, where plants like Henry are grown in sequence to enrich the soil, rather than deplete it. Henry was amazed to see how his fellow plants supported each other, creating a thriving, biodiverse environment.

But the most exciting part of Henry's visit was yet to come. After spending a day at the farm, learning about sustainable agriculture, Henry was taken to a green factory, where the magic of transformation would occur. This factory was a place of innovation, where environmental responsibility was the cornerstone of production.

Inside the green factory, Henry witnessed the remarkable processes by which hemp plants like him were transformed into a multitude of eco-friendly products. First, he saw his fibers being spun into strong, durable thread, which was then woven into clothing. This clothing wasn't just stylish; it was breathable, biodegradable, and produced with a fraction of the water and energy used to make traditional textiles.

Next, Henry watched in awe as other parts of him were molded into biodegradable plastics. These plastics, unlike their petroleum-based counterparts, would break down naturally, returning to the earth without harming it. Henry felt a surge of pride knowing he could be part of the solution to the plastic pollution problem.

But the surprises didn't end there. Henry was then taken to another part of the factory, where his pulp was being turned into paper. This paper was strong and smooth, perfect for writing, drawing, and even packaging. And best of all, it was made without the need to cut down trees, preserving forests and the creatures that called them home.

Throughout his adventure, Henry was filled with joy and amazement at the endless possibilities that he and other hemp plants offered. He realized that his journey from the meadow to the sustainable farm and green factory was a testament to the economic potential of hemp. By embracing sustainable practices and innovative technologies, humans could create a world where economic growth and environmental stewardship went hand in hand.

As Henry returned to the meadow, his heart was full of hope and excitement for the future. He had seen firsthand how plants like him could play a crucial role in building a more sustainable and economically vibrant world. And he couldn't wait to share these stories with all who visited the meadow, inspiring others to dream of a greener, more prosperous planet for generations to come.

-Henry's elconuomiclis adventury...
It's a call to action

Henry's economical adventure was more than just a journey; it was a call to action, a reminder that each of us has the power to make a difference through the choices we make and the products we support. And as the stars twinkled above the meadow, Henry the Hemp stood tall, a beacon of sustainability and economic innovation, lighting the way toward a brighter, greener future.

HENRY THE HEMP
Henry's Global Journey

The dawn of a new adventure had arrived for Henry the Hemp, one that would take him across the vast oceans and skies to explore the corners of the Earth. This journey was not just about discovery; it was a mission to connect with people and cultures around the globe, sharing the universal story of hemp's incredible potential. With a map in his roots and a heart full of excitement, Henry embarked on a global journey that would unveil the richness of cultural exchange and the unifying power of sustainable practices.

As the sun kissed the horizon, Henry's first stop was the rolling hills of China, a land with a deep historical connection to hemp. Here, in the birthplace of hemp cultivation, Henry learned about ancient techniques passed down through generations. He visited fields where hemp was grown just as it had been thousands of years ago, providing fibers for clothing, ropes, and even paper. In bustling markets, Henry shared stories with artisans who revered hemp for its durability and sustainability. This exchange of knowledge was a testament to the enduring legacy of hemp in human civilization.

From the East, Henry's journey took him to the heart of Europe, where hemp was experiencing a renaissance in innovation and design. In countries like France and Germany, Henry marveled at modern uses of hemp, from bio-composites used in car manufacturing to hempcrete in sustainable construction. He engaged in workshops and discussions about the future of eco-friendly materials, witnessing how traditional knowledge and cutting-edge science were blending to create a sustainable future. This leg of the journey highlighted the global shift towards greener alternatives and the role of cultural collaboration in driving change.

Next, Henry ventured to the vibrant landscapes of Africa, where he was introduced to the critical role of hemp in community development and sustainable agriculture. In Kenya and South Africa, Henry saw how small-scale hemp farming empowered communities, providing sustainable livelihoods and improving soil health. He learned about the challenges and triumphs of hemp cultivation in diverse climates and how, through sharing practices and innovations, communities could thrive while protecting their natural heritage. This experience underscored the importance of global trade and knowledge exchange in addressing environmental and economic challenges.

Crossing the Atlantic, Henry arrived in North America, where he explored the dynamic world of hemp entrepreneurship and research. In Canada and the United States, he visited universities where students and scientists were exploring the frontiers of hemp technology, from water purification systems to energy-efficient batteries. Henry engaged with startups that were pushing the boundaries of what hemp could do, creating products that amazed and inspired. This leg of the journey was a celebration of innovation, showing how creativity and collaboration could lead to groundbreaking solutions for global issues.

Finally, Henry's journey brought him to the lush landscapes of South America, where indigenous communities shared their ancestral knowledge of hemp with him. In countries like Chile and Brazil, he learned about hemp's role in traditional medicine and its potential for ecological restoration. These conversations about sustainability and respect for the earth were a poignant reminder of the wisdom that indigenous cultures hold in protecting our planet.

MATTHEW PETCHINSKY
Throughout his global journey, Henry witnessed the incredible diversity of hemp's uses and the shared commitment to sustainability that transcended borders and cultures. He saw how global trade and cultural exchange, rooted in respect and collaboration, could spread innovative solutions and foster a more sustainable world.

As Henry returned to the meadow, his map was filled with stories of people and places, all connected by the green thread of hemp. His journey was a mosaic of experiences that illustrated the power of unity in diversity. Through his tales, Henry taught us that our global future depends on our ability to learn from each other, to trade not just goods, but ideas and dreams for a sustainable future.

MATTHEW PETCHINSKY

Henry's global journey was not just an adventure; it was a call to action for all of us to embrace the principles of sustainability, innovation, and cultural respect. In the interconnected world of Henry the Hemp, every thread of knowledge and every exchange of ideas brought us closer to a greener, more harmonious planet.

Conclusion: Henry's Message to the World

MATTHEW PETCHINSKY
As the sun dipped below the horizon, painting the sky in hues of orange and pink, Henry the Hemp stood in the center of the meadow, his leaves rustling softly in the evening breeze. The adventures of the day had brought laughter, learning, and a sense of wonder to all who had joined him. Now, as the stars began to twinkle in the twilight sky, Henry gathered his friends—the children, the animals, and the plants—for one final story, a message not just for those in the meadow, but for the world.

Henry began with a dream, a vision of a planet where the green of the forests matched the green in the hearts of its people. A world where rivers flowed clean and clear, where the air was fresh and filled with the songs of birds. In this dream, cities were verdant with rooftop gardens and streets lined with trees, where people lived in harmony with nature, not apart from it.

Henry's voice, gentle and persuasive, carried across the meadow, urging everyone to listen, to understand the profound bond that exists between humans and the natural world. "But for this dream to come true," Henry continued, "it requires more than just plants. It needs you—each and every one of you—to play your part."

MATTHEW PETCHINSKY
Ask questions, Leaarn;
about the plants aninals
that share your home.
He spoke directly to the children, his leaves shimmering under the moonlight, encouraging them to be curious about the world around them. "Ask questions," he urged. "Learn about the plants and animals that share your home. Discover how everything in nature is connected, and how you can help protect it."

Treat the Earth as you would you'ur best friend,
Anpranp ellh rmereut of pestruce of a futurare genrations,
are pmgmemen peempy e pespect your our only friend.

Henry emphasized the importance of respect — respect for nature, for each other, and for future generations. "Treat the Earth as you would your best friend," he said. "With kindness, with care, and with love. Remember, we only have one planet, and it's up to all of us to take care of it."

HENRY THE HEMP
As Henry's message came to a close, the meadow was filled with a sense of hope and determination. The children, inspired by Henry's words, promised to carry his message with them, to share the dream of a greener, healthier planet with others.

And so, under the watchful eye of the stars, Henry, the Hemp whispered a final wish into the night, a wish for a world where humans and nature lived in perfect harmony, thriving together on this beautiful planet we call home.

Educational Aspects of "Henry the Hemp: The Plant of Wonders"

In creating a story that captivates and educates, "Henry the Hemp: The Plant of Wonders" aims not just to entertain but to enlighten. Within its pages, children and adults alike are invited on a journey of discovery, learning about the incredible world of hemp through the eyes of Henry. To enhance this educational journey, here are detailed educational aspects, including a glossary of simple terms related to hemp and fascinating facts that can spark curiosity and learning.

Glossary of Simple Terms

- **Hemp:** A type of plant that is part of the Cannabis sativa species. Unlike some other types of cannabis, hemp has very low levels of THC (the compound that makes people feel "high") and is grown for its fibers, seeds, and oils, which have various uses.
- **Sustainable:** A method or resource that can be maintained or kept up over time without harming the environment or depleting natural resources.
- **Biodegradable:** Something that can be broken down naturally by microorganisms like bacteria and fungi, turning back into natural substances like water, carbon dioxide, and compost.
- **Eco-friendly:** Products or practices that are not harmful to the environment.
- **Crop Rotation:** The practice of growing different types of crops in the same area in sequenced seasons to improve soil health, reduce soil erosion, and prevent disease and pests.
- **Biocomposite:** A material composed of biological (often plant-based) and synthetic components, used to create environmentally friendly alternatives to plastics and other materials.
- **Hempcrete:** A building material similar to concrete but made with hemp fibers, which is sustainable and has good insulation properties.
- **Textiles:** Materials made by weaving or knitting fibers together. Hemp fibers can be used to make textiles for clothing, bags, and more.

Fascinating Facts About Hemp

1. **Ancient Use:** Hemp is one of the oldest known crops used by humans, with evidence of its use dating back over 10,000 years. It was used for textiles, paper, and even as food.
2. **Strength and Durability:** Hemp fibers are among the strongest and most durable of all natural textile fibers. Products made from hemp, such as ropes and textiles, are known for their longevity and resistance to wear and tear.
3. **Environmental Benefits:** Hemp plants have a rapid growth rate and require less water and no pesticides to thrive, making them a more sustainable choice compared to traditional crops. They can also absorb carbon dioxide more efficiently than many trees, contributing to the reduction of greenhouse gases.
4. **Versatility:** Hemp can be used to make over 25,000 different products, ranging from textiles, bioplastics, and building materials to health foods, beauty products, and biofuels.
5. **Soil Health:** Hemp has deep roots that help prevent soil erosion, improve soil health by replenishing vital nutrients, and even remove toxins from contaminated soil in a process known as phytoremediation.
6. **Legalization and Regulation:** The legal status of hemp has varied globally and historically. Recent changes in legislation in many countries have recognized hemp's agricultural and industrial potential, leading to a resurgence in its cultivation and use.
7. **Nutritional Value:** Hemp seeds are highly nutritious, rich in essential fatty acids (Omega-3 and Omega-6), protein, vitamins, and minerals. They can be eaten raw, ground into a meal, sprouted, or made into dried sprout powder.

Through "Henry the Hemp: The Plant of Wonders," readers are invited to explore these educational aspects, enriching their knowledge and appreciation for hemp and its role in sustainable living. The glossary and facts presented serve as a foundation for a lifelong journey of curiosity and respect for nature, encouraging children to become thoughtful stewards of our planet.